I Am Your
Evil Twin

Look out for more books in the Goosebumps Series 2000
by R.L. Stine:

I Am Your
Evil Twin

R.L. Stine

Hippo

Scholastic Children's Books,
Commonwealth House, 1–19 New Oxford Street, London WC1A 1NU, UK
a division of Scholastic Ltd
London ~ New York ~ Toronto ~ Sydney ~ Auckland
Mexico City ~ New Delhi ~ Hong Kong

First published in the USA by Scholastic Inc., 1998
First published in the UK by Scholastic Ltd, 1999

ISBN 0 590 11381 X

Typeset by Rowland Phototypesetting Ltd, Bury St Edmunds, Suffolk
Printed by Mackays of Chatham plc, Chatham, Kent.

10 9 8 7 6 5 4 3 2 1

"Here we are—home," Uncle Leo said. He pulled into the driveway of a big, run-down brick house and switched off the engine.

"The old place hasn't changed at all since we were kids, Leo!" Mum exclaimed. She raised her eyebrows. "Except that the weeds are taller. And the vines are thicker."

"I don't have much time for gardening. I'm always in my lab," Uncle Leo admitted. He peered at me through his thick glasses. "I hope you'll be happy here, Montgomery."

That was when I knew it was going to be a long year.

My name is Montgomery Adams. My mum actually believes *Montgomery* is a good name for a kid. "It's what your father wanted," she always says. My dad died a month before I was born. "Besides, it's elegant."

I don't want to be elegant. I want to be normal. It's hard enough when you're a tall, skinny twelve-year-old who has red hair and a sort of big nose.

But when your name is Montgomery, normal goes right out of the window.

I hadn't seen Uncle Leo since I was about six. When he picked Mum and me up at the Philadelphia airport, the first thing he said to me was, "You must be Montgomery." His voice was deep and sort of hollow.

"Yeah. Everyone calls me Monty," I told him.

He kept calling me Montgomery anyway.

Uncle Leo climbed out of the car and strode towards the house. Mum and I followed, lugging our bags.

"Look, Monty. There's the tree where we had our rope swing." Mum pointed to an old maple by the side of the house. "I bet Leo has some rope, if you want to make another one. Oh, you're going to love it here."

I peered suspiciously at the maple tree. "It looks dead to me," I muttered. "The house doesn't look too alive, either."

"Stop being so negative, Monty." Mum frowned. "This is an adventure."

An adventure. Right.

Mum is a zoologist. She works for a university. In a couple of months, she's going off to spend a year in the jungles of Borneo, studying orang-utans. The university gave her loads of money to do it. She is really excited. Mum loves adventures.

I *hate* adventures. All I want is a normal life.

Mum can't take me with her, because there are no good schools in the jungles of Borneo. Instead, she was planning to stick me with her brother—my uncle Leo.

Which would be fine. Except that Uncle Leo is not normal. He does some kind of weird science. He's a professor—Professor Matz. But he doesn't teach. He does research. He works in his lab all the time. And he lives in this huge wreck of a house in the dinky little town of Mortonville, outside Philadelphia.

And he calls me Montgomery.

"It's too bad Nan isn't here this weekend," Mum remarked as we went inside.

"That's true," I muttered. Uncle Leo's house might not seem so bad with Nan around.

My cousin Nan is Leo's daughter. She's cool— and nothing like her father. She spends most summers in California with us, while Uncle Leo travels round the world doing his weird science.

Nan and I have a lot in common. We're the same age. We both have single parents—Nan's mum died when she was two. And we both play the piano.

She's good at sport—better than I am—but she doesn't rub my face in it. And she's funny. We like the same jokes.

3

"Nan is away at music camp until August," Uncle Leo explained. He glanced at me. "Your mother tells me you're quite a talented piano player yourself, Montgomery."

We walked into the living-room, a huge, shabby place with faded brown furniture. I sniffed. The air smelled funny—a combination of mould and something sour and chemical. Yuck.

"What are you working on, Leo?" Mum asked, settling into one of the brown armchairs. "Anything earth-shattering?"

Uncle Leo's cheeks flushed. "Oh, this and that," he mumbled.

Mum laughed. "You're so hush-hush about your work," she teased. "Like one of those mad scientists from the movies."

I studied Uncle Leo. He *did* look like a mad scientist, with his thick glasses, bony face and wild tufts of reddish hair. He was tall and stooped, and he wore a short-sleeved blue shirt with a plastic pocket protector.

Yes. I could definitely picture him in a lab, cackling and rubbing his hands over beakers of bubbling green liquid.

SCREEE! Something creaked over my head.

I jumped. "What was that noise?"

"Just the house settling," Uncle Leo answered. "It's old. Old houses do that."

"Or maybe it's one of the *Others*," Mum suggested. "Remember, Leo, how you and I used to believe there was a whole other family that secretly lived in the attic?"

"Maybe *you* believed it," Uncle Leo muttered. "I never did."

I sank into the musty sofa and sighed. A mad scientist and this creepy old house.

It was going to be a long year.

I had a hard time falling asleep that night. The house kept creaking around me. Some of the noises sounded almost like human voices. Growling, moaning.

Finally I did fall asleep. For a minute.

I woke up to the sound of a shrill squeal. I squinted around the room. What was that bright light glaring in my eyes?

Hey! I wasn't in my bed any more.

I seemed to be in a hospital operating room!

My heart began to pound. What was going on?

A tall, thin figure loomed over me. A man. But I couldn't see his face because of the light shining in my eyes. All I could see was the outline of his head. He wore a surgical cap and mask.

He held up a gloved hand. A piece of metal glittered in his grip.

My eyes widened in horror.

A scalpel!

I tried to sit up.

I couldn't move!

"Help!" I shouted.

But no sound came from my throat!

"Relax," the man in the mask said. His impossibly deep voice boomed in my ears. It sounded like a worn, stretched cassette tape.

My heart raced. I wanted to jump up. To run. But I couldn't make my body obey me.

This is a nightmare! A horrible nightmare!

That's when it hit me.

It *was* a nightmare!

Yeah! That's it, I thought.

I'm dreaming. This isn't real.

That's why I can't move. Or speak.

It's a dream. That's all. Just a dream.

My heartbeat began to slow down.

And then the man in the mask lowered the scalpel to my ear—and began to scrape it across my skin.

"No!" I yelled with all my strength. "Nooooo!"

And suddenly, I could move. I bolted up in bed, gasping.

Sweat poured down my cheeks.

I stared around.

I was back in a dark bedroom. A guest room in Uncle Leo's house.

The man with the scalpel had gone.

The door swung open. "Monty?" Mum called. "Are you all right? I thought I heard you call out."

"I think I was dreaming," I managed. "Sorry if I woke you."

"Don't worry about it. Go back to sleep," Mum advised.

I lay back down. I stared at the ceiling while my racing heart slowed down.

I closed my eyes.

But it was a long time before I fell asleep again.

*

I went home for the summer. In October, Mum left for the jungle. Uncle Leo picked me up at the airport. He wore another blue short-sleeved shirt with a plastic pocket protector. Or maybe it was the same one. I couldn't tell.

It was a cool, clear autumn day. The leaves on the trees were just starting to change colour.

Mortonville looked pretty. But I still felt nervous.

As we pulled into the driveway, the front door of Uncle Leo's house opened. My cousin Nan stepped out on to the porch.

"Hi!" she yelled, running up to the car. "You're here at last! Has Aunt Rebecca left? Don't you wish you could go to Borneo with her?"

Nan was as tall as me, and thin. She wore baggy jeans and a blue hooded sweatshirt. Her hair, a lighter shade of red than mine, hung in a long, single braid down her back. Her green eyes sparkled from under a thick fringe.

"Hi!" was all I managed before she began chattering away again.

"Come on in," she urged, leading me inside. "Did Dad show you round the house when you last came to visit? I bet he didn't. Dad always forgets stuff like that. Oh, well, I'll show you. It's a cool house. You'll like it." She rolled her eyes. "Except the hot water doesn't always work very well."

In the living-room, Uncle Leo cleared his throat. "Montgomery, I have a little present for

8

you," he announced. "Just something to welcome you to our house."

I stared at him in surprise. A welcome present? I never would have expected something like that from Uncle Leo.

He reached into his jacket pocket and pulled out something small and silvery. He held it up for me to inspect.

I peered at it. It was a pin, shaped like an eight-point star. As Uncle Leo moved his hand, a rainbow of soft colours played across the surface of the star.

"Wow. What is that stuff?" I asked.

"Dad invented it," Nan explained proudly. "It's a new kind of glow-in-the-dark material. You know. For people to put on their bikes and jogging clothes et cetera. He made me a pair of earrings shaped like moons. Isn't it neat?"

"It's really cool," I agreed, staring at the pin.

"I'm working on lots of cool things, Montgomery," Uncle Leo said. He peered at me through his glasses. "I wish I could tell you about them all."

He stood there a moment, gazing at me with his head tilted to one side. I felt my ears start to turn red.

What is he staring at? I wondered.

Then Uncle Leo seemed to shake himself. "Here, let me pin it on for you," he suggested. Stepping forward, he reached for a fold of my T-shirt.

"That's okay." I brought my hands up quickly. "I can—OW!"

I felt a sharp pain in my index finger.

Uncle Leo had jabbed the pin into it!

I stared at my hand. A drop of bright red blood welled up from the puncture.

"Oh, my! I am so sorry, Montgomery!" Uncle Leo whipped out a handkerchief and dabbed at the blood. "Are you all right? Really, I'm very, very sorry. That must have hurt."

"I'm okay," I mumbled. My finger throbbed. And I wished he would stop fussing. "It's no big deal. Anyway, thanks for the pin. I really like it."

"He's fine, Dad," Nan assured Uncle Leo. "Come on, let's go into the kitchen. I saw a bag of doughnuts in there."

"Of course." Uncle Leo handed me the pin. Then, tucking his handkerchief back into his pocket, he strode towards the kitchen. Nan and I followed him.

"A new bakery opened in town last week. They bake fresh doughnuts three times a day," Nan explained. "They were still warm when we bought them."

She crossed to the worktop and pulled a box out of a white paper bag. As she lifted the top, a delicious cinnamon aroma filled the air. My mouth began to water. Breakfast on the plane seemed a long time ago.

"How about some apple juice to wash them

down?" Uncle Leo opened the refrigerator and took out a large jug.

"Sounds great," I declared, taking a seat at the wooden breakfast table. Uncle Leo might be weird, but at least he wasn't a health nut like Mum. She never bought doughnuts.

Nan set the box on the table. I picked out a doughnut and bit into it. Mmmmm! It was still a little bit warm on the inside. The sugar and cinnamon crunched against my teeth.

I gobbled down the rest of the doughnut in about three bites. Then I took a big swig of apple juice.

I gazed round the kitchen. It was big and cheerful, with green-and-white-checked lino on the floor and green curtains at the window.

It's not so bad when Nan is here, I thought happily. I reached for a second doughnut.

That's when I started to feel strange. Very strange.

My stomach clenched as if someone had just punched me. Waves of hot and cold spread through my body.

My throat closed. I couldn't breathe.

My stomach clenched again.

My ears buzzed.

What's wrong? I wondered dizzily.

What is happening to me?

I sat at the table, swaying. My ears rang.

"Monty, are you okay?" Nan asked. "You look a bit pale."

"I . . ." I groaned. "I don't feel . . ."

I leaned forward. My stomach heaved.

And I threw up all over the green-and-white kitchen floor.

Nan jumped up from her chair and backed away. "Yuck!" she groaned.

"Montgomery! What on earth . . . !" Uncle Leo cried.

I straightened up in my chair, feeling a little better. I stared in horror at the hideous mess on the floor. "I—I'm sorry," I stammered.

I was so embarrassed. My face was on fire. I felt like crawling under the table and staying there. For the rest of the year.

Uncle Leo fetched a mop and bucket and began cleaning up the mess. "Are you ill?"

"Maybe you need a doctor," Nan chimed in.

"No. I'm all right," I mumbled. "Really."

In fact, I felt much better. I even thought I knew what had made me throw up.

I picked up the doughnut bag and studied the label. Underneath the name of the bakery was a list of ingredients. I found the one I was searching for right away.

"It's the doughnuts," I explained. "They're fried in peanut oil."

Nan slapped her forehead. "Oh, no! You're allergic to peanuts! I didn't even think of that. Poor Monty!"

"Yes, indeed," Uncle Leo agreed quickly. "I'm so sorry, Montgomery. You walk into the house. First I stab you, and then I poison you! What a beginning."

"It wasn't your fault," I protested, embarrassed. "You didn't know. Um—I'd better brush my teeth."

"You remember where the toilet is? The second door on the left, upstairs," Nan told me. "When you come down we can make sandwiches for lunch. *Not* peanut butter and jelly," she added with a grin.

I went up and splashed water all over my face and brushed my teeth. By now I felt perfectly fine—except that I wished I hadn't made such an idiot of myself.

I stepped out of the toilet and walked down the long hallway. Even in the middle of the day, it

13

was dark and shadowy. The floorboards creaked as I moved. The hall was lined with wooden doors—at least five on each side. All closed.

Why did Uncle Leo need such a huge house? It was just him and Nan—and me, now. What did three people need with all this space?

What was behind all those doors?

At the far end of the hall, I spotted a low, arched doorway. Peering in, I saw that it led to a back staircase. Where does that come out? I wondered.

I started down the narrow, steep stairs. *CREAK! CREAK!* The worn treads felt as if they were bending under my feet.

I hope the whole thing doesn't collapse under me, I thought nervously. Then I'd *really* be off to a great start with Uncle Leo.

A moment later I reached the landing at the bottom. I seemed to be in the back of the house now. Through a doorway on the left, I glimpsed Uncle Leo's study. A room next to it contained a piano and a couple of armchairs.

In front of me, across the hall, I saw another door. Unlike the other doors in the house, this one was metal, and painted bright white.

And it stood open, just a tiny bit.

What's in there? I wondered. I reached for the doorknob.

"Don't!" a voice growled in my ear. "Don't ever go in there!"

My heart gave a hard *THUD*.

I spun round—and found myself staring at Uncle Leo.

"I—uh—" I didn't know what to say. Did he think I was snooping or something? "I think I'm lost."

"I understand. It's a big house," Uncle Leo rumbled. "I didn't mean to sound harsh. It's just that this door leads to my lab. Many of my experiments are very delicate—and some are quite dangerous. I wouldn't want you to get hurt, Montgomery."

"Um—right." All I wanted at that moment was to get out of there. Uncle Leo was giving me the creeps.

"The kitchen is that way." Uncle Leo pointed down the hall. Then he opened the lab door and vanished inside.

I thought I heard a bolt slide shut behind him.

Weird, I thought, as I hurried down the hall. Definitely weird.

That afternoon, Nan took me to a car park where kids went to Rollerblade. I liked Nan's friends. Especially a girl called Ashley. She was kind of cute, with straight, shoulder-length dark hair and big brown eyes. She laughed at my jokes. And she was the best Rollerblader there.

On Sunday it rained. Nan and I hung around the house. We spent a while in her room, playing games on her computer. Then we decided to go downstairs and see what was on TV.

We walked down the first-floor hall, past door after door. The house creaked and groaned around us. Thick, shifting shadows hung in the grey light.

"So what's behind all those doors?" I asked.

Nan shrugged. "Bedrooms, mostly. The house has ten of them. I think it used to be an inn or something."

"It's creepy," I complained. "I keep getting confused and forgetting which room is mine. And the house makes all these weird noises. It always sounds like there are people sneaking around behind my back."

"You mean Dad didn't tell you?" Nan stared at me.

"Tell me what?"

"About . . ." Nan's voice trailed off.

"About what?"

Nan drew a deep breath. "About . . . about the mutants. They live in this house with us," she explained. She lowered her voice. "They only come out at night. They can't stand light."

The back of my neck prickled. "Stop kidding around."

"I'm serious!" Nan insisted. "Why do you think we have all those extra bedrooms?"

"But—but—where do they come from?" I sputtered. "How come your dad lets them stay here?"

"They're experiments that went wrong," Nan whispered. "Dad feels responsible for them, I suppose."

I stopped walking. My eyes went wide. "Whoa!"

Then I noticed a grin creeping across Nan's face.

"You believed me! You really believed me!" she cried.

I scowled. "Very funny. I did not."

"Yes you did!" she crowed.

"No way. Who would believe such a lame story?" I grumbled.

"It was a good story. Don't be such a sore loser, Monty. You know I won't tell anyone."

I hoped she wouldn't. Especially not Ashley.

Nan led me down the back stairs. Past Uncle Leo's lab and into the room with the piano. That was also where the TV was.

17

Low, muffled noises came through the wall from the lab. What was Uncle Leo *doing* in there?

"Have you ever been in your dad's lab?" I asked Nan in a low voice as we sat down.

"Only once. Dad is very strict about that, you know," Nan told me.

"I noticed," I muttered. "So what happened?"

"I was about seven," Nan recalled. "I sneaked in one day while Dad was taking a nap. I was sure there would be all kinds of freaky experiments. Two-headed rabbits and stuff."

"Yeah? Were there?" I asked.

Nan shook her head. "Just a load of test-tubes and charts. It was boring. But before I could get out, Dad woke up. I knew I'd be in huge trouble if he caught me there. So I hid in the supply closet. It was awful! I must have been in there for two hours. And I *really* had to go to the toilet. Finally Dad left—and I managed to slip out."

She laughed. "I've never tried to sneak in again."

I picked up the remote and clicked the TV on. "How come your dad always calls me Montgomery?" I asked, flipping channels.

Nan shrugged. "I don't know. Dad's weird that way," she remarked. "Formal." She reached over and grabbed the remote from me. "Give me that! I hate the way you flip channels. You go so fast I can't tell what anything is."

18

"I wish he'd call me Monty like everybody else," I grumbled.

"Hey, look!" Nan poked me in the side with the remote. "The *Twilight Zone* movie! I love this movie. I've seen it four times."

I'm not crazy about scary movies. But I wasn't about to tell Nan that. She'd just call me a wimp.

I leaned back on the sofa and thought about better names for me.

"This is the best part," Nan whispered. "Are you watching?"

"Dave," I said.

"Huh?" She stared at me. "What are you talking about?"

"Dave," I repeated. "What do you think? 'Dave Adams'. It has kind of a ring to it."

Nan snorted. "Don't be an idiot."

"Well, what about Paul?" I asked. "Do I look like a Paul to you? I think I look like a Paul."

"I think you look like an idiot," Nan replied. She glanced back at the TV. A commercial was playing. "And you made me miss the best part of the movie!"

"So what? You've seen it four times already," I pointed out. "Hey—how about Alan?"

"Shut up, Monty." Nan poked me with the remote again. "Go and make some popcorn."

"You make it!" I objected.

"I don't want to miss the movie," Nan declared.

19

So I headed for the kitchen. I found a bag of popcorn and stuck it in the microwave.

"Hurry up, Monty!" Nan yelled from the TV room. "It's starting again!"

"Big whoop," I muttered.

When the popcorn was ready, I dumped it into a bowl and went back to the TV room.

As I passed the door to the lab, I heard Uncle Leo's voice inside. "No!" he cried. "No, it's impossible."

There was a moment of silence. Then I heard a voice—but it spoke too softly for me to make out any words.

I paused by the door. Who was he talking to in there?

I caught my breath as Uncle Leo's voice rang out again.

"No!" he shouted. "No! You're insane! Do you hear me? Insane!"

The back of my neck prickled.

Who was Uncle Leo yelling at? *Who* was insane?

I hadn't seen anyone else in the house—and I'd been here all day.

What was going on in that lab?

"Monty! Get in here!" Nan yelled.

I stepped into the TV room and shut the door behind me.

I cleared my throat. "Nan—your dad is screaming at someone in his lab," I told her.

Nan shrugged. "Dad gets quite emotional about his work," she said without taking her eyes off the TV.

"But who is he talking to?" I demanded. "Who is in there with him?"

Nan turned to stare at me. Then she broke into laughter.

"Hello! What century are *you* from, Monty?

Haven't you ever heard of the phone?" she asked.

"Oh." I felt my face grow hot with embarrassment.

The phone. Of course. Uncle Leo was talking on the phone.

I thought I'd heard two voices. But obviously that was impossible.

I flopped down on the sofa beside Nan. "Here," I offered, passing her the bowl of popcorn.

I settled back to watch the rest of the movie.

But I had a hard time concentrating. I kept thinking of Uncle Leo's voice. Of the way he shouted "You're insane!"

I don't care what Nan says, I thought. I don't care if he was on the phone.

Uncle Leo is really strange.

"Well, this is it—Taft Middle School," Nan announced.

I gazed up at the long brick building. It looked pretty much like my old school in California, except that it was bigger. Same rows of metal-framed windows with dirty white shades, same rectangle of scrubby grass in the front.

Even though the day was dark and misty, kids hung around on the grass, talking and throwing Frisbees before classes began.

"You're in Ms Eckstat's tutor group," Nan

said, studying my printed schedule. "Too bad you're not in Mr Schneider's with me. Ms Eckstat is all right, but she's pretty strict."

"That's okay. I'm not exactly a troublemaker," I pointed out.

I was nervous. It's hard enough starting a new school. But starting a month after everyone else is even tougher.

The bell rang. We hurried inside. Nan pointed out my classroom on the ground floor. "I'll meet you in the canteen later," Nan promised. "Good luck!"

"Thanks." I gazed after my cousin as she hurried to her own class.

I tried to look casual as I walked into my classroom. Ms Eckstat gave me a nod and a smile. She was in her fifties, I guessed, with curly grey hair cut short and glasses that hung on a chain round her neck.

Nan's friend Ashley was in my tutor group. Her dark hair was pulled into a pony-tail, and she wore a sweatshirt that said PENN STATE. I tried to catch her eye, but she was in the middle of a conversation with another girl.

I glanced round the room. There were several empty seats. "Where should I sit, Ms Eckstat?" I asked.

Ms Eckstat frowned. "You know where to sit, Montgomery," she said. "I assigned you a seat last week, when you came to see me."

I stared at her for a second, blinking. See her? Last week?

"Um—excuse me, Ms Eckstat," I began, "but I wasn't here last week. This is my first day."

Ms Eckstat put her hands on her hips and sighed. "Stop fooling around, Montgomery, and take your seat."

I turned towards the class and scanned the seats. Ashley pointed to a chair near the windows.

"Don't argue," she whispered. "Just sit down."

I stumbled to the middle row and sank into the seat. A chubby kid in the back sniggered in a mean way.

Ms Eckstat started writing on the blackboard. I tried to pay attention, but it was hard.

What was Ms Eckstat talking about? I hadn't been to Taft Middle School until today. I'd never met any of the teachers.

Last week I was still in California.

So why did she say she'd talked to me?

That afternoon I had my first piano lesson. I was studying with Nan's teacher, Mr Schneider. He's also the school music teacher.

I'm a pretty good player, but today it took me a while to warm up. I was rattled.

I kept thinking about Ms Eckstat mixing me up with another kid. There weren't any kids who looked like me in my class. I was the only redhead.

Mr Schneider leaned over the piano and frowned. He was bald, except for a fringe of wiry hair round the sides of his egg-shaped head. He wore a striped sweater over a polka-dot tie.

"Try again," he instructed when I messed up my scales for the second time. "At this rate, I don't know if you'll be ready for the school assembly next week."

"What school assembly?" I glanced up at him, startled.

"Didn't Nan mention it? Next Friday's

assembly will showcase student musical talent," Mr Schneider explained. "She says your playing is on the same level as hers. I thought maybe the two of you could play a duet."

That could be fun, I thought. And maybe Ashley would be impressed, if I played really well.

Maybe my new life in Mortonville would start getting better. It had been pretty strange so far.

First Uncle Leo practically killed me with those doughnuts he bought. Then my teacher yelled at me for not remembering something that never happened. And those voices I heard in the lab . . .

I needed something normal in my life. And what's more normal than a piano recital?

"Let's get to work!" I declared, and attacked my scales again.

The rest of the lesson went well. Mr Schneider smiled and nodded as I breezed through my exercises. "Good, very good," he kept saying.

Finally he gave me a pile of sheet music and sent me home. "Good work! But keep practising, Monty," he called after me from his doorway.

I hurried home. I took the porch steps two at a time. "Nan? Uncle Leo?" I called as I walked into the empty kitchen. "Hello?"

No one answered me. Then I remembered— Nan was babysitting for a kid down the block.

Uncle Leo must be in his lab, I thought. I suppose he can't hear me in there.

I hurried down the hall to the lab. I grasped the knob and pulled the door open.

"*Shut that door!*" someone screamed from inside the lab.

I was so startled I let the door go. It banged shut.

That wasn't Uncle Leo's voice! It wasn't even a man's voice. It was too high.

Someone else was in his lab.

But who?

A moment later the door swung open. Uncle Leo stepped out. His face looked even paler than usual. There were dark circles under his eyes.

"Did you need something, Montgomery?" he asked.

"I—uh—" I felt flustered. "I didn't mean to bother you."

"It's all right." Uncle Leo gave me a wide grin. It looked really weird on his bony face. "I'm sorry I snapped at you. Next time, please remember to knock."

"*You* snapped at me?" I blurted out. "But that wasn't your voice, Uncle Leo."

"Of course it was," Uncle Leo insisted. He cleared his throat. "I may have sounded a bit, ah, tense. I was in the middle of a very delicate experiment."

"But . . ." My voice trailed off. I felt very confused.

I turned away. "Sorry to bother you," I mumbled.

"It's all right," Uncle Leo repeated. "Better get started on your homework."

"Right."

Uncle Leo whisked back inside his lab. I headed towards the kitchen. I needed a snack. And I needed to think.

I was almost positive the voice that screamed at me wasn't Uncle Leo's.

Was Uncle Leo lying to me?

Why?

What did he have to hide?

The next day, school started pretty well. I made everyone at my lunch table laugh with my imitation of our gym teacher, Mr Mason. He's really short and walks like a duck. A muscle-bound duck.

Ashley was there. She laughed really hard.

Sixth period I had art. When I walked into the art room, the first person I spotted was Ashley. She grinned and pointed to the seat next to her.

All right! I thought as I crossed to her table. Things are looking up!

I recognized a couple of other kids in the class too. Vinny Arnold, another of Nan's friends, sat near the door. And Seth Block, the big kid who had laughed at me in tutor time, was at the table next to ours.

"Good afternoon," the teacher, Ms Braun, called. She was a wispy-looking woman with long brown hair that kept escaping from its bun and straggling into her eyes. "Today we'll continue to explore shapes and colours in three dimensions. I've set up papier-mâché tubs and paints at every table. Be creative, people!"

I glanced over at Seth's table. He and two other boys were already building something huge and lumpy out of papier-mâché.

"Hey, boys—how's your project going?" Ms Braun asked them.

"Ours is the coolest," Seth boasted. "It's a volcano. We're going to paint it so it looks like there's real lava pouring down the sides. And we're going to make little tiny bodies of people who got caught in the flow. *Ahhh! I'm burning!*" He clutched his throat and began to make horrible faces.

Ashley rolled her eyes. "He is such a jerk." She picked up a brush and began to dab blue paint on the mask she was making.

"What are they making?" I whispered to her. "Seth's head?"

Ashley cracked up. "It isn't lumpy enough to be his head!" she replied.

I scooped some papier-mâché out of the tub and began to mould it around my hand. "I'm going to make a life-sized model of myself. What do you think so far?"

"Not lumpy enough," Ashley said with a grin. She plunged her hand into the papier-mâché tub and slapped some glop on my hand. "There. That's better."

"Hey!" I protested. I grabbed another paint-brush and swirled a big red circle on the cheek of her mask. "How about some nice rosy cheeks?"

"You want rosy cheeks? I'll give you rosy cheeks!" Ashley dipped her brush in the red paint. Before I could stop her, she painted a red circle on *my* cheek.

"All right, you asked for it." I reached for the jar of green paint.

"No way!" Ashley exclaimed when she saw what I was doing. She grabbed at my arm. I jerked away.

I think I must have pulled a little too hard.

WHACK! My arm slammed into the row of paint jars. They flew off the table—and shattered on the floor.

Except for the yellow paint. *That* went all over Seth's table. All over Seth's model volcano.

Shocked silence fell over the room.

Ashley and I stared at each other in horror.

Then everyone started talking at once.

"You're history!" Seth growled. He balled his right hand into a fist and glared at me.

"Way to go, Monty!" someone else called.

Ms Braun hurried over. She glared down at us with her hands on her hips.

"Look at the mess you've made," she scolded. "And the paint you've wasted!"

"Sorry," I mumbled. "It—it was an accident."

"Well, I *hope* you didn't do it on purpose!" Ms Braun snapped. She sighed. "I'd better call the caretaker to clean up all this broken glass. Until then, please be very careful where you walk, people."

She turned and gave Ashley and me another glare. "I want you back in here after school. You're going to clean up this entire art room. Maybe that will teach you some respect for the materials."

I ducked my head. "Yes, ma'am."

"This stinks! I have soccer after school," Ashley complained as Ms Braun walked away. She scowled at me. "Why did you have to be so clumsy?"

Me? If she hadn't grabbed my arm, I wouldn't have knocked the paints over.

But I was too embarrassed to argue.

It was only the second day at my new school. And already I'd got into trouble twice.

"Sorry," I said again.

For the rest of the class, Ashley and I worked in silence. Ashley got fresh paints and painted her mask. I tried to make an alligator out of papier-mâché, but it ended up looking like a sausage with legs.

After my last class, I headed back to the art room to meet Ashley. I flung open the door— and stared in horror.

The room was a complete wreck.

Rainbows of paint spattered the floor, the walls, the windows, the furniture. A tub of papier-mâché had been emptied over the teacher's desk. Drawing paper had been yanked off the shelves and ripped into confetti.

It looked as if someone had beaten the papier-mâché projects with a baseball bat. I glimpsed Seth's volcano. It was completely smashed. So was my alligator. And everything else.

Ashley stood in the middle of the mess, staring at it. I took a step inside.

"Huh? What happened?" I murmured.

Ashley wheeled round. She was crying.

"Stay away from me!" she cried. "You're crazy!"

"What are you—" I began, bewildered.

"I saw you!" Ashley cried. "I saw you, Monty! Why did you do this?"

"Me?" I stared at Ashley in confusion. "What are you talking about?"

"You wrecked the entire art room!" Ashley shrieked. "Why did you do such a stupid thing?"

"But—but I didn't!" I protested. "I didn't do this! I wasn't even here!"

"How can you say that?" Ashley aimed a finger at me. "I saw you! I saw you smash all this stuff. Then you climbed out of the window."

"It's not true!" I cried. "I swear, Ashley, you're wrong. It wasn't me. I've just got out of science class. I didn't do this."

Ashley wiped her eyes with a tissue. "Are you going to try to blame *me* for this?"

"No! I know you didn't do it. But I didn't, either! I swear!"

"But I saw you!"

I put a hand to my forehead. "This is really weird!"

Ashley looked past me towards the door. "Ms Braun!" she gasped. "I—um—"

I whirled round.

"What happened here?" the art teacher demanded.

I froze, my mouth hanging open. Ashley stared at her feet.

"Well?" Ms Braun insisted. "Ashley, are you responsible for this mess?"

"No," Ashley replied.

"Monty?" Ms Braun asked.

"No!" I cried, a little too loudly.

Ashley took a deep breath. "I saw Monty do it," she mumbled.

The art teacher stepped towards me from the doorway. She shook her head.

"Ashley, you may go. Monty, I'm taking you to the head teacher's office," she told me. "Right now. Let's go!"

"Mrs Williams will see you now," the secretary announced.

I gulped. I'd hardly ever been sent to the head before.

Especially for something I didn't do!

Ms Braun put a hand on my shoulder and steered me into Mrs Williams's office. "I'm afraid we have some trouble here," she declared.

The head was a tall, heavy-set woman in a grey suit. She wore her black hair cut very short.

As she glanced up at me, her stern dark eyes narrowed.

"So you're back again," she remarked. "I'm not surprised. I told you this morning that smart mouth of yours would get you into trouble."

She turned her gaze to Ms Braun. "What has he done this time?"

My jaw dropped. I stared at Mrs Williams in shock.

This morning?

I wasn't in her office this morning!

I'd never even *seen* her before!

What is going on?

Angrily, Ms Braun began to tell Mrs Williams about the mess in the art room.

I listened in shock.

Am I going crazy?

Did I really wreck the art room—without knowing it?

Did I get sent to the head's office this morning? If I did, how come I can't even remember it?

No way! It's impossible!

With a shiver I remembered what had happened the day before. When Ms Eckstat insisted she'd met me last week.

Something really weird was going on.

"It wasn't me!" I burst out. "Honestly, I didn't do it. I didn't do any of it!"

Both women stared at me. Mrs Williams shook her head.

"We know you did it, Monty," she pointed out. "Another student saw you. Unless you can tell us why Ashley would lie about something like that."

"I don't know!" I cried. "But I know I didn't do it. And I've never been to your office before, Mrs Williams. I've never even met you before!"

Mrs Williams studied my face as if she couldn't believe what she was hearing.

"I know it's hard, Monty," she said quietly. "I know it's not easy adjusting to a new school and a new home."

I bit my lip. I wanted to scream. No matter what I said, she'd never believe me.

"But this behaviour is unacceptable," she went on. "And lying about it only makes things worse."

"I'm telling the truth!" I insisted.

Mrs Williams shook her head. "I'm willing to give you one more chance. But this lying must stop. Go back to the art room and clean up that mess. And I don't want to see you in my office again."

I trudged back to the art room, shoulders slumped.

This is a nightmare! I thought. What is happening to me?

I found cleaning supplies in a cupboard and got to work. This is going to take hours, I realized. It's so unfair!

I gathered up the rubbish on the floor and

threw it away. With a sigh, I started scrubbing the paint off one of the walls.

Then, out of the corner of my eye, I caught a sudden movement in the window. I glanced to my right.

My own face stared in at me—wiry red hair, big nose, everything.

My heart stood still for a moment.

Then I realized I was simply seeing my reflection in the window glass.

Get a grip, Monty! I told myself. I turned away and started scrubbing again.

Another flash of movement at the window. I glanced round sharply. Was there someone out there?

Again, I found myself staring at my reflection.

It seemed awfully sharp and clear. Maybe because the day was so dark, I thought. I frowned.

My reflection frowned.

Weird. I noticed something squinty about my eyes. A sly gleam. Do I really look like that? I wondered.

I stuck out my tongue.

My reflection stuck out its tongue.

I raised my left hand and waggled my fingers.

My reflection didn't move.

My mouth fell open. I dropped the scrubbing brush and moved to the window.

A loud clattering noise made me jump.

The room was plunged into darkness.

I glanced wildly round the darkened room.

Ms Braun stood by the window. She held the cord of the venetian blind in her hand. The blind was down now—covering the window.

Hiding my reflection.

Ms Braun frowned at me.

"Why are you staring out of the window?" she demanded. "You should be cleaning! You've hardly made a dent in this mess."

"I—I—" I stammered. "My reflection! It—"

I broke off. How could I explain.

"Stop fooling around, Monty," Ms Braun snapped. "Get back to work."

She gave me one last angry stare. Then she turned and strode towards the door.

"I'll be back in an hour," she warned.

I barely heard her. I was still picturing my reflection—my reflection that didn't move.

An hour later, I dumped the last bucketful of dirty water down the sink and gazed round the art room.

It looked better, but not perfect. I hadn't been able to get all the paint off the walls. Faint blue and red streaks still stained them.

But I'd done my best. I grabbed my books from my locker and started to walk home. I hoped Nan would be there. I needed to talk to her.

I felt as if I were going crazy!

Long shadows stretched across the pavement. A chilly breeze stirred the leaves over my head. I quickened my pace as I passed a vacant plot. Nan and Uncle Leo were probably wondering where I was.

SNAP! A twig cracked somewhere behind me.

I glanced over my shoulder. Was there someone back there?

The pavement seemed empty.

I kept walking. I was only a few blocks from home now. But as I passed under a big maple tree, I heard a snigger behind me.

I turned round and peered into the shadows.

There! A dark shape darted behind a thick tree trunk.

My heart began to pound.

Someone is following me.

Maybe it's the person who set me up in the art room!

Maybe now I'll find out what's going on.

I adjusted the straps of my rucksack. I pulled my Dodgers cap lower on my forehead.

"I know you're there!" I yelled. My pulse was racing. "Why don't you come out where I can see you?"

For a moment nothing happened. Then someone stepped out from behind the tree.

Seth.

A second later, Vinny and Rob, his two buddies from art class, came out from behind other trees. For the first time I noticed how big they both were. At least as big as Seth.

Twice my size.

And there were *three* of them. You do the maths.

They stepped towards me. Surrounded me.

Seth made a fist. He ground it into his palm.

Uh-oh. I gulped.

"Wh-what's up?" I asked. I meant to sound cool. But my voice came out all squeaky.

"You know what's up," Seth growled.

"You smashed our volcano," one of his friends accused me. "Ashley told us."

"It took us three weeks to build it," the other one said.

"So now we're going to smash you," Seth muttered.

42

"Oh, no," I groaned.

"Please." I tried to smile. "You're making a big mistake. I didn't—"

That was as far as I got—before they all jumped on me.

"Nooo!" I threw my arms up to cover my head.

"Hold his arms!" Seth instructed his buddies.

I struggled wildly. But it was no use. All I got was a torn shirt and a punch in the nose.

Blood trickled down my cheek. I could already feel my nose swelling up. Great. Now it would look even bigger than usual.

Seth and his friends high-fived one another, then ran away.

Ten minutes later I limped up the drive to Uncle Leo's house. I had a moustache of dried blood. My nose throbbed. My ribs ached.

I walked inside and slammed the door behind me. I could hear Nan practising the piano in the back of the house.

"Is that you, Monty?" she called as I started up the stairs.

"Yeah," I muttered.

"Come in here! We should practise our duet."

I didn't answer. I didn't even slow down.

I didn't feel like seeing anyone. Not even Nan. I didn't feel like explaining how I got beaten up for something I didn't even do. I just wanted to hide in my room.

Better yet, I wanted to board the next plane out of Mortonville.

Borneo was sounding better all the time!

On Monday morning I had English third period. Ms Eckstat, my tutor, was also my English teacher.

I got to class a little late. Ms Eckstat gave me a stern look as I hurried to my seat. The one by the window.

I settled myself in and pulled out my books.

"Can anyone tell me what a proper noun is?" Ms Eckstat asked. "Let's see . . . Monty?"

"Uh—" Why did she have to call on me? I hate grammar! Especially early in the morning. I searched around in my brain.

"Uh—is it a person, place, or thing?" I tried.

Ms Eckstat folded her arms. "Yes—but which one?"

Uh-oh. I could feel myself starting to sweat. I glanced nervously round the room.

My gaze caught on the window—where my own face grinned back at me.

For a second I thought I was staring at my reflection in the glass again.

Then I realized I *couldn't* be seeing my reflection.

The window was wide open!

There was a kid standing outside, staring in at me.

And he looked exactly like me!

I jumped up from my seat. "Hey!" I burst out.

"What's the matter, Monty?" Ms Eckstat demanded.

I didn't reply. I couldn't stop staring at the kid outside the window. My double.

He gave me a mocking grin. "What's the matter, Monty?" he whispered.

Then he turned and ran.

"Hey!" I shouted again. I didn't even stop to think what I was doing.

I leapt out of the window—and ran after him.

He sprinted towards a clump of trees. "Stop!" I yelled as I tore across the lawn. "Come back here!"

Who was he? Where was he going?

"Monty!" I heard Ms Eckstat call behind me. "Monty—come back this minute!"

I ignored her and raced up a small hill.

But when I reached the top, my double was nowhere in sight.

"No!" I cried. How could I have lost him? Frantic, I scanned the lawn. The clump of trees.

Nothing. He had completely vanished.

I bent down and rested my hands on my knees, trying to catch my breath. Could he have ducked back into the school? I wondered.

I turned towards the brick building. And spotted the open window of my classroom.

"Oh, no!" I gasped.

Ms Eckstat was framed in the window. So was about half my class. They were all staring and pointing at me.

What had I done? How could I explain?

Maybe someone else had seen the double. Maybe someone would back up my story.

I jogged back across the lawn. This time I went round to the front doors. I figured Ms Eckstat wouldn't want me to climb back in through the window.

As I hurried to class, I kept an eye out for my double. But there was no one else around. My footsteps echoed through the deserted halls.

Ms Eckstat met me at the classroom door, with folded arms. "What was *that* all about?" she demanded. She was getting pretty fed up with me, I suppose.

"I'm sorry, Ms Eckstat. But I saw something really—" I began.

She cut me off. "I don't know what kind of rules you have at school in *California*," she

48

snapped, "but around here we don't jump out of the window and run around whenever we feel like it."

"I know. But—" I tried again.

"You know?" Ms Eckstat interrupted. "Well, if you know the rules, then I don't understand your behaviour at all. Or were you trying to be funny?"

"No!" I cried, horrified. "I—"

"Because if that's the case, I should warn you that clowning around won't get you anywhere in my class," Ms Eckstat said severely.

"But Ms Eckstat—"

Ms Eckstat frowned. "I've heard enough, Monty. Go back to your seat. And remember, I've got my eye on you."

Heard enough? She hadn't let me say anything at all!

Everyone stared at me as I slunk down the aisle to my desk. Whispers and sniggers followed me.

And I still hadn't found out anything about that kid who looked just like me. My twin.

My twin! How could somebody look so much like me?

Who was he? Where did he go?

And why was he trying to ruin my life?

"So what happened?" Nan whispered as we moved up the hot-lunch queue. "Everyone is talking about how you went nuts in English class this morning."

I set a plateful of lasagne on my tray. "Have you ever seen a boy round here who looks like me?" I asked.

Nan frowned. "Not really," she admitted. "I mean, there's Gus Halloran. He has red hair—but he wears it in a crew cut. And he's quite fat."

"No. I mean a *lot* like me." I glanced round the canteen. "*Exactly* like me. Like my twin or something."

Nan's frown deepened. "No. There's no one at this school who looks that much like you."

I drew a deep breath. "Well, this morning during English some kid who looks exactly like me stared in at the window. So I chased after him to find out who he was. Only he disappeared."

I grabbed a milk from the cooler. "And no one else saw him but me."

"No way!" Nan laughed. "Get serious."

"I *am* serious. Very serious," I insisted. "I'm telling you, this really happened."

"Come on!" Nan scoffed. She led me towards a table. "Maybe it was just some stranger passing by who sort of looked like you. Or maybe it was some weird kind of mirage or something."

"No," I insisted. "He spoke to me! He was real! And you know what else? I think he must be the one who trashed the art room and mouthed off to Mrs Williams. That's why everyone thinks it was me—because he looks just like me!"

Nan's green eyes went wide. "Monty, do you know how crazy you sound? A kid who looks just like you who's going around getting you into trouble?"

Nan shook her head. I could tell she thought I was making it all up.

But I knew what I had seen.

And I also knew who I had to ask about it. Uncle Leo.

There's only one answer, I thought.

I must have a twin. A twin that Mum never told me about.

Uncle Leo will know. He's Mum's brother.

He has to tell me!

I raced home after my piano lesson that afternoon. I hurried through the house to the kitchen.

Uncle Leo was there, pouring himself a cup of coffee. I noticed that his hands were shaking slightly.

When he caught sight of me, he seemed to give a start. Coffee splashed out of his cup on to the worktop.

"Montgomery!" He frowned. "Has school finished already?"

"Uncle Leo." I planted myself in front of him. "I have to know. Tell me the truth. Do I have a twin?"

51

Uncle Leo gasped. His face slowly turned a fiery red.

"How did you find out?" he whispered.

I gasped. I felt as if all the air had been knocked out of me.

"You mean it's true? I *do* have a twin?"

Uncle Leo gazed at me. Then, slowly, he lowered himself into a kitchen chair.

"Yes, you do. It's a sad story," he said in a low voice.

"What is?" I slid into the chair opposite him. "Please, Uncle Leo. Tell me!"

Uncle Leo cleared his throat.

"What you must understand, Montgomery, is that twelve years ago, your mother was very young—and very poor," he began. "Your father had just died, leaving her alone. She was a student. She had no job, no money—nothing. She didn't even have a house to live in. Just a tiny little apartment on the university campus."

"Okay, okay. I get the picture," I said impatiently. "Go on!"

"When you and your twin were born," Uncle

Leo continued, "it was the happiest day of her life—but also the saddest. You see, she knew that she couldn't possibly feed and care for two children by herself."

Uncle Leo sipped his coffee and gazed into his cup. "Your mother thought long and hard about it," he told me. "But finally she had to accept the truth. The best thing she could do for both of you children was to send one of you away. To someone who could care for you properly."

He gave a little shrug. "You were the first-born, Montgomery. By ten minutes. She kept you and sent your twin away."

I sat there staring at the table. I hardly knew what to think. My whole world seemed to be turning upside down.

"Wow!" I murmured finally. "This is *wild*!"

"I'm sorry you had to find out this way. Your mother was going to tell you herself—on your thirteenth birthday," Uncle Leo explained. He paused. "How *did* you find out?"

I glanced up. "I've seen him. He lives somewhere in this town. Isn't that amazing?"

"He?" Uncle Leo repeated. His face filled with confusion. "No, no. Your twin isn't a boy, Montgomery." Uncle Leo leaned forward. "Nan is your twin!"

"*Nan?*" I cried. I gaped at Uncle Leo. "*Nan* is my twin?"

"Of course!" Uncle Leo nodded. "I thought you understood that. Your mother didn't want to give her daughter to a stranger. And your Aunt Susan and I always wanted children of our own. I've raised Nan as my own daughter all these years. But she isn't. She's your twin sister."

"But—but—" I sputtered. I put my hand to my head. I felt so confused!

"Does she know?" I asked after a moment.

"No, she doesn't. Not yet," Uncle Leo replied. He cleared his throat. "I was going to tell her on her thirteenth birthday too, just like your mother. But now I suppose she has to know. I'd like to tell her myself. Alone, if you don't mind. It will be . . . well, a shock."

"Sure." I nodded. The news was bizarre enough to me. I couldn't even imagine how it would hit Nan. The man she had always thought of as her father . . . was her uncle!

And she had a brother—*me*!

Talk about a shock.

I felt a surge of happiness for a second. I have a sister! A twin sister! And it's Nan!

It was quite cool. But it was also really weird. All this time I had a twin and didn't know it.

What else was going on that I didn't know about?

I started to feel as if I couldn't trust anybody. How did I know what was real? Or what was the truth?

The really strange thing was, Uncle Leo still hadn't answered my question.

"But what about this kid I saw who looked just like me?" I asked Uncle Leo. "Who was that?"

Uncle Leo frowned. "I don't know anything about that," he muttered. "It must be a coincidence." He stared off into space for a moment.

"Uncle Leo?" I prompted.

He seemed to shake himself. "Yes, it's a coincidence. That's all."

"But—" I began.

We both jumped as the front door slammed. "Hello?" Nan's voice called out. "Anybody home?"

Uncle Leo and I exchanged quick glances. I stood up.

"I'm going," I whispered.

I ran for the back stairs. Let Uncle Leo give Nan this bizarre news in private. I had some thinking to do, anyway.

My life was getting weirder by the minute.

"It's still so hard to believe," Nan murmured. "You aren't my cousin—you're my brother. And Dad isn't Dad—he's Uncle Leo. And Aunt Rebecca is Mum." She shook her head.

It was past midnight. Nan and I sat on her bed, talking. We'd been talking for hours already.

"You have to admit it explains a lot," she added. "Like how come we're both good piano players."

"Maybe. But we don't really look that much alike," I argued. "I mean, we both have red hair, and we're both tall and skinny, but—"

"But I'm much better looking than you," Nan broke in. She grinned at me. "We're fraternal twins, not identical twins. Boy-girl twins are never identical, dummy."

"Hey—watch it." I punched her shoulder. "Remember, I'm your older brother."

"By a whole ten minutes. Big deal," Nan scoffed.

"Hey. You know what should have tipped us off?" I said.

"The fact that we have the same birthday?" Nan teased.

"Well—yeah. But I mean, besides that. Remember the summer we were seven, when we went to that birthday party at that kid Evan Seymour's house?"

"The really spoilt kid with the crooked teeth?" Nan asked.

"Yeah. And remember how he got that cool model train set for a birthday present?" I went on. "And then at the end of the party, the engine and the caboose were missing and no one could find them?"

"Yeah . . ." Nan eyed me. "So?"

I leant forward. "Well, I stole the engine," I told her, lowering my voice. "I just thought it was the coolest thing I'd ever seen. I had to have it. And later, when I went into your room to get something, I found the caboose in your desk drawer."

Nan's cheeks turned red. "Are you kidding? You mean you knew I took that caboose and you never said anything?"

"What was I going to say?" I asked. "I took the engine. I couldn't say anything or I might have got caught myself." I shrugged. "Besides, I never liked Evan."

"Yeah. He was a jerk," Nan agreed.

We both burst out laughing.

"I can't believe it," Nan gasped. "We both had the same guilty secret all these years!"

"So, are you—are you angry with Mum?" I

ventured at last. "I mean, because she didn't keep you."

Nan frowned and glanced down. She played with the end of her long red braid.

"I don't know," she said after a moment. "I mean, it feels really weird when I think about it. That she knew all the time that I was her daughter, but she never said anything."

I shook my head. "I still can't believe it. But if it makes you feel better, I know she loves you. She always talks about how great you are and everything."

She shrugged. "I know. Aunt Rebecca—I mean, Mum—" She shivered. "It sounds so strange! Mum. Anyway, she's always been incredibly nice to me. I've spent almost every summer with you lot. She calls and writes letters to me all the time. I suppose I feel as if she really loves me. Even though she couldn't keep me."

She paused. "What am I going to say to her next time I see her? When she comes back to get you?"

I thought that over. "I don't know. We have a long time to think about it."

I kicked the heel of my shoe against the floor. My head was so full of questions I thought it would explode.

"How about Uncle Leo?" I added. "Are you angry with him for not telling you sooner?"

Nan shook her head. "I was at first. But now—I mean, he's my dad. I love him. I'll always think of him as my dad. Knowing that he's really my uncle doesn't change that. And he did plan to tell me when I turned thirteen."

I yawned. "Well, I'd better go to bed." I stood up and strode to the door. "See you in the morning—Sis."

"Yuck!" Nan made gagging noises. "I don't care if you are my brother. Don't ever, *ever* call me that again! It is *so* lame!"

I laughed and closed the door behind me.

As I passed the phone in the hall, it rang.

Weird. Who would call at this hour?

I picked up the receiver. "Hello?"

"You're going to get it now," a boy's voice threatened.

"Huh?" I frowned. "Who is this?"

"You're going to get it," the voice repeated. "Things are going to get tough, Monty. Very tough. Starting now."

15

"Who is this?" I whispered into the phone. "What are you talking about?"

CLICK!

"Hello? Hello?"

No answer.

No one there.

I stood there in my pyjamas, clutching the receiver in my hand. A chill swept over me.

Who was that on the phone?

What did he mean, things were going to get tough?

What was he going to do to me?

"Are you nervous?" Nan whispered.

"A bit. What about you?" I whispered back.

"Very," she admitted.

It was the next Friday. Nan and I were waiting backstage in the school auditorium. We were about to play our piano duet for the assembly.

I glanced at my blue button-down shirt and

khaki trousers. They looked okay. No food stains or anything.

Four days had passed since I'd got that weird phone call—but nothing had happened. Yet.

Probably Seth, I figured. Just playing around, giving me a hard time for wrecking his volcano.

What if it wasn't Seth?

Somebody had already started messing with my life. Pretending to be me. Getting me blamed for things I hadn't done.

What if it was my double?

The head was finishing up her announcements. Nan and I were on next. Better make sure I have all my music, I thought. I opened my black plastic folder.

My stomach lurched.

The folder was empty. Completely empty.

"Oh, no!" I gasped. "My music! It isn't here!"

"What?" Nan grabbed my arm. "You moron! Did you leave it at home?"

"No! I checked my folder three times before we left the house," I insisted. I snapped my fingers. "It must be in my locker. Maybe it fell out of the folder or something. I have to go and get it."

"But we're going on in five seconds!" Nan whispered frantically. "What am I supposed to do?"

"Stall them. Play a solo. I don't know!"

I raced through the wings and down the hall.

Of course, my locker was at the far end of the building. It figured.

I skidded up to my locker and twirled the dial desperately. "Twelve—seven—eleven," I mumbled under my breath as I spun the little wheel.

I squeezed the latch. The metal door swung open. I stared into the locker.

My jacket hung on a hook. My books were stacked on the shelf.

No sheet music.

I tugged the books out of the locker. I pawed frantically through them. Was the music inside my notebook?

No. Not there.

I had no idea where it was.

Maybe I'd lost it in the hall somewhere, I thought. Or left it in the toilet.

I stumbled through the halls, staring at the floor. No sign of my music.

I turned a corner and saw an open door. I paused for a second to peer into the room.

Just a supply room.

But before I had a chance to turn round, someone gave me a quick, hard shove.

OOF! I landed on my belly on the floor. The door slammed shut. The room went dark.

"Hey!" I cried.

CLICK! A key turned in the lock. I sprang to my feet and yanked on the door.

Someone had locked me in!

"Let me out!" I shouted. I banged on the door with my fists.

No one answered.

"Open this door!" I yelled. "Let me out! Now!"

I set my ear to the door and listened. Not a sound.

I felt a sudden cold lump in my stomach.

Someone had locked me in here on purpose, I thought. Why?

I tried the door again. It didn't budge.

What am I going to do?

I sniffed. Then I coughed. There was a sharp, bitter scent in the air. And it seemed a bit smoky in here.

After a moment I realized the smell—and the smoke—was coming from a puddle of an oily-looking liquid. More of the stuff oozed out of a plastic jug that lay on its side on the floor.

"Ohhh," I moaned.

And then I began to cough.

I bent over double, hacking and wheezing.

A thick grey cloud poured out of the mouth of the jug on the floor.

"No!" I gasped.

The fumes from that jug! They're choking me!

I can't breathe.

Can't breathe!

16

I clutched my stomach, coughing and gagging.

"Help!" I tried to cry. But I couldn't choke the word out.

I banged on the door. But no one came to let me out.

Clouds of toxic smoke rose up from the jug on the floor.

This is serious! I realized. If I don't get out of here soon, I'll pass out.

I might even die!

I peered round the little room frantically. Struggling to see. The smoke made my eyes water and burn.

But I could make out the rectangle of light from a little window. A little window near the ceiling. It was the kind that latched at the top and pulled down.

It was higher than my head. Can I climb through it? I wondered.

I have to. I don't have any choice!

I staggered over to the window. I saw a stack of metal rubbish bins in a corner. I dragged one under the window and turned it upside down. Then I climbed on top of it.

The fumes were much thicker up high. I pulled my shirt up to cover my mouth and nose.

I grabbed the latch on the little window and pulled with all my strength.

"Come on," I panted. "Come on. Come on."

POP! At last it sprang open. The window swung down and banged against the concrete wall. One of the panes shattered. But I didn't have time to worry about that.

Coughing, I seized the edges of the window-frame and hauled myself up. My arms shook.

I'm not going to make it, I thought.

I don't have the strength to pull myself through!

And then my head was outside and I was breathing in gulps of fresh air.

I hung there for a moment, just sucking it into my lungs.

Then I dragged myself the rest of the way through the little window. It was a tight fit. "Ow!" I cried out as my trousers got stuck on a nail. I yanked and yanked until they ripped free.

At last I was out. I sprawled on the grass, gasping. Greyish smoke trickled out of the little window and floated away with the breeze.

After a few seconds, I felt strong enough to

climb to my feet. I limped towards the front entrance of the school.

I was sure I'd missed my chance to play the duet with Nan. I didn't care. I was glad to be alive.

I stumbled towards the auditorium with a sick feeling in my stomach. I coughed again. My lungs felt as if they'd been scrubbed with sandpaper.

I slipped backstage. I heard the sound of a piano playing, then applause.

Nan had started without me, I realized.

I stepped into the wings to watch. Nan stood in front of a piano, taking a bow.

Then I noticed something else. *I* was on-stage too.

I gaped in amazement at a kid on-stage who looked just like me!

He had my hair. My nose. My long, thin face.

He even wore khakis and a blue button-down shirt.

He and Nan bowed to the audience together. I stared, frozen in horror.

She thinks he's me! I realized. My own cousin—I mean sister!—thinks that's me on-stage with her!

He's pretending he's me!

Who *is* he? Why is he doing this?

I had to find out. Now was my chance.

A whole auditorium of people watched. They'd

all see that I had a double. At last, they would believe me.

"Hey!" I yelled from the wings.

My double spun round. Our eyes locked.

I made a move to the stage. But my double leapt towards the baby grand piano—and shoved it as hard as he could. It rumbled across the stage like a speeding Mack truck.

Roaring at me!

I stood for a second with my mouth hanging open in shock.

He was trying to kill me—with the piano!

The piano shot towards me. It was going to crush me. I was trapped!

At the last second, I dodged to the side.

The piano thundered past. I felt the wind as it went by.

It smashed into the back wall with a jargling *CRACK*.

I sagged against the wall, panting.

From the auditorium, I heard gasps, then shouts. I caught a glimpse of Nan's shocked face as she stared into the wings. Her mouth was wide open.

My double ran past me as I stood there.

He was laughing!

"Hey!" I yelled. I tore after him. "Come back here! Come back!"

My double pounded down the empty hall. I raced after him.

"Stop!" I screamed. "What are you doing? Who are you?"

My double rounded the corner. He was heading for the front doors! He was getting away!

I gritted my teeth and tore round the corner after him.

And suddenly I was face to face with him!

I stumbled to a halt. My chest heaved.

"Who—are—you?" I panted. "Who?"

The boy with my face gave me a mocking smile.

"Do you want to know the truth about me?" he asked.

"Yes!" I cried. My voice echoed in the hall.

"You think you're so tough," he breathed in my face. "Well, you're not. I'm better than you. And I'm going to prove it."

My double took a step towards me.

Then he hauled his fist back and punched me in the stomach. Hard. Harder than I'd ever been punched before.

I doubled over, gasping for air. Red spots danced in front of my eyes.

I glanced up at him through blurry eyes.

"I'm taking over your life, Monty," he said softly. "And you can't stop me. That's all you need to know."

He turned and jogged to the front doors.

I tried to stumble after him. But I had no strength in my legs. I couldn't seem to draw a deep breath.

My knees buckled. I slumped to the floor.

My head whirled.

And everything began to go black.

I'm about to pass out! I realized dimly.

"No!" I groaned.

I can't!

I have to follow him. Find out where he lives. Who he is.

I have to stop him before he completely ruins my life!

Gasping, I hauled myself to my feet. I staggered through the school doors.

Outside, I propped myself against the side of the building and sucked in air. It was growing easier to breathe.

I scanned the street in both directions. Which way did he go?

There! I spotted a flash of red hair turning the corner. I stumbled after him. He was about half a block ahead of me.

I'm going to trail that boy if it kills me, I thought. How could somebody look so much like me? And what did he mean, he was going to take over my life?

My double didn't seem to be in any big hurry. He didn't realize I was following him. He picked up a stick and trailed it along the wrought-iron fences. *CLANG! CLANG! CLANG!*

Then he threw the stick away and pulled something out of his pocket. I couldn't make out what it was.

He shook it, then aimed it at a car. A dark cloud hissed out.

Spray paint! I sucked in my breath. My double was spray-painting the side of a car!

Man, was this kid bad news!

If I didn't stop him—soon—he wouldn't just get me kicked out of school. He'd get me sent to jail!

I hurried forward—and accidentally kicked a bottle on the pavement. It rolled clattering into the gutter.

My double turned his head sharply.

"Whoa," I muttered. I ducked behind a tree. Had he seen me?

I counted to ten, then peeked round the thick trunk.

No. He hadn't spotted me. He made a final pass with the spray-paint can. Then he stuck it back in his pocket and continued on his way.

I followed. But when I got to the car he had spray-painted, I stopped and stared in horror.

He had painted a giant red heart on the door of the white car. Inside the heart were the words MONTY LUVS ASHLEY 4EVER.

"Oh, no," I groaned.

I untucked the tail of my shirt and tried to rub the paint off. Too late. It was dry.

I knew Ashley walked home this way. Half the school walked home this way.

They would all see it.

They would all believe I wrote it.

And there was nothing I could do about it.

"Aargh!" I pounded my fist on the bonnet in frustration. Then I took off after my double again.

I had to stop him!

I trailed him down three more blocks.

When he turned left on Chester, I began to wonder.

He was taking the same route home that I did.

Where did this kid live, anyway?

He crossed Chester at the traffic lights and started up my block.

This is too weird, I thought. He can't possibly live on the same block as me. Nan or Uncle Leo would have noticed.

Halfway up the block, my double turned right. Into the driveway of Uncle Leo's house.

"Huh?" I gasped.

I couldn't waste time hanging back half a block any more. I sprinted up the street. Cut across the lawn.

And skidded to a stop. My mouth fell open in horror.

My double was climbing into the kitchen window of Uncle Leo's house!

18

"No way!" I cried.

Why was he going to my house?

Had he already convinced Uncle Leo he was *me*? Nan fell for it—why not Uncle Leo?

What if Uncle Leo thought *I* was the double—and kicked me out? He really *would* be living my life!

I ran up the porch steps, digging in my pocket for my key. I jammed it into the lock and threw the door open.

"Uncle Leo?" I yelled. I charged towards the kitchen. "Uncle Leo! Look out for that kid. He's not me! He's not Monty!"

Silence.

Then I remembered. Uncle Leo was at school today. He'd come to watch Nan and me play our duet.

I burst into the kitchen and stared wildly around.

Empty. The room stood empty. The curtains

at the open window billowed softly in the breeze.

Where did he go? Where was my double? What was he doing here?

I raced through the house, checking all the rooms.

He wasn't in the living-room. Or the dining-room. Or the TV room.

I stuck my head into Uncle Leo's study. No one there. A screensaver of chemical formulas marched across his computer monitor.

I ran up to the first floor. Tore down the hall, throwing open the doors to all the bedrooms.

Nothing.

I couldn't find him anywhere. I even checked the attic.

Finally, panting, I plodded down the front stairs.

Where could he have gone? Had he sneaked out of the house while I was searching the first floor?

What was he up to?

The door burst open just as I reached the bottom of the stairs. Nan ran in.

"Monty!" she cried when she caught sight of me. "What is the matter with you? Are you completely crazy? Why did you smash the piano? Why?"

I grabbed her arm. "Nan, listen. You have to believe me!" I cried. "That wasn't me! I swear it wasn't me! I was backstage—I saw the whole thing. I'm telling you, I really do have a double! He's the one that smashed the piano! He's evil!"

"Cut it out," Nan snapped. "This isn't funny!"

"I'm not joking! Why won't you believe me?" I begged.

"You say you have a double who looks like you—and dresses like you too?" Nan crossed her arms. "Do I look like a moron?"

"He's my double. My twin. I swear! It's not impossible. Think about it. I'm *your* twin, and you didn't know it until a week ago."

Nan's eyes widened. "Are you saying—oh, wow!"

I nodded. "Nan, what if we're not just twins? What if we're triplets?"

Nan put a hand to her forehead. "This is too weird," she murmured. "Come on. Let's ask Dad."

"Uncle Leo? Isn't he at school for our recital?"

Nan was already hurrying down the hall. "He never showed up," she called over her shoulder. "He was writing a paper for a science magazine this morning. I bet he got all involved in his work and forgot to come."

She pushed open the door to Uncle Leo's study and strode in. "Dad?"

"He isn't here," I said, following her in. "I looked."

"Maybe he's in the lab." Nan bit her lip. "We

have to go in there and talk to him. We have to find out the truth!"

I turned to leave the room.

That's when I caught sight of the paper lying on top of Uncle Leo's printer. Its title leapt out at me.

THE FUTURE OF CLONING by Dr Leo E. Matz.

I gasped. For a moment the room seemed to swim before my eyes. I clutched the edge of the desk.

"Nan," I croaked. "Look at this!"

Nan turned back and peered at the paper. "So?"

"Don't you get it?" I cried. "The double is a clone! He cloned me. Uncle Leo cloned me!"

"Cloned you? Wow. Now I *know* you're losing it," Nan exclaimed. "Even if he could do it—which he can't—my father would never clone you."

"How do you know?" I shot back.

Nan glared at me. "I just know. He wouldn't do a sick thing like that!"

"But it all fits!" I argued.

Everything was falling into place in my mind. "Remember when Uncle Leo gave me that pin—and he poked my finger with it? And then he whipped out his handkerchief and wiped up all the blood? I think he was getting a cell sample or something!"

"He was not!" Nan's green eyes flashed. "I can't believe you, Monty. He was just trying to be nice to you."

"But my double appeared just a few days later," I pointed out. "A few days after Uncle Leo wipes up my blood with his handkerchief, a kid appears who looks exactly like me. And when I follow him, he comes back to *this* house. How do you explain *that*?"

Nan's face set in a scowl. "I don't know. But I know my dad didn't clone you," she said. "You're wrong, Monty. Dead wrong. And I'm going to prove it to you."

I folded my arms. "How?"

"I'm going to ask him. Right now," Nan declared. "Come on. He's got to be in his lab. Let's go."

She whirled round and marched towards the white metal door.

I followed her a little more slowly. I was terrified of facing Uncle Leo.

But I had to know the truth.

Had Uncle Leo really cloned me?

Nan yanked open the door to the lab and stepped in. I was right behind her.

She stopped so suddenly that I crashed into her. I heard her gasp.

Then I saw what she was staring at. And I gasped too.

Uncle Leo faced us. He wore a white lab coat.

Next to him stood my double.

Next to that double stood *another* double.

And another. And another.

There were *four* exact copies of me in Uncle Leo's lab.

The four clones smiled at me. "Hi, Monty," they sang out.

"I don't believe this!" I gasped.

I felt as if I were going insane!

Uncle Leo glared at us. "I warned you never to come in here!" he snapped.

Nan took a step forward. "But . . . but, Dad . . . why?" she cried. "Why did you do this to Monty?"

Uncle Leo straightened to his full height.

"I am a scientist," he declared. "I can't worry about one boy's silly problems. With my cloning project, I am going to change the world. For ever."

"No!" I shouted. "You can't! I—"

Uncle Leo frowned. "I'm sorry. I hoped it wouldn't come to this. But I can't allow you two to spoil things."

He turned to the clones. "Get them!" he

barked, pointing at Nan and me. "Don't let them escape!"

Instantly the clones spread out around the lab.

"Dad! No!" Nan wailed.

I swallowed hard. What were they going to do to us? How could Uncle Leo turn against us like this?

The clones edged closer.

We had to get out of there. Clutching Nan's arm, I began to back towards the door.

"Where are you going, Monty?" one of the clones called. He leapt behind us to the door. He slammed the bolt shut.

We were locked in!

They surrounded us. Nan and I huddled together.

Think! I told myself. *Find a way out!*

The clones circled us. The circle tightened.

"Get away from us!" Nan pleaded. "Leave us alone!"

Two of the clones made a grab for me. I dodged away—and dived to one of the lab worktops. I grabbed a beaker full of clear liquid.

The clones surrounded Nan and blocked the door.

"Get back," I warned. "Away from the door. Or I'll throw this in your faces."

The clones laughed. "Go ahead!" one of them urged. "It's tap water."

Water! In a lab beaker?

Maybe he was bluffing.

Desperately, I hurled the beaker at the clones. "Nan—look out!" I called.

The clones ducked. Nan too. The beaker shattered against the door.

"Stop that!" Uncle Leo called sharply. "You're destroying expensive equipment!"

One clone seized Nan by the arms. She struggled fiercely. "Let go of me! Let go!"

I started towards her. "Leave her alone!"

Another clone marched up to me and grabbed my arms. "You can't win. Don't even try to fight us," he sneered.

"No!" I gasped. I ripped one arm free. "Hi-ya!" I karate-chopped the clone's wrist and yanked my other arm free. Ducking away, I crouched and ran under a stainless-steel table.

That is, I *tried* to run under the table. But I didn't duck low enough.

WHACK! I rammed my head against the rounded metal edge.

I fell backwards. "Ohhhhh," I moaned.

"Monty!" Nan gasped.

It was all over. Two of the clones grabbed me on the lab floor. They dragged Nan and me over to the supply closet.

Then they opened the door and shoved us in. I heard a key turn in the lock.

I stared into the darkness. A faint light

washed in from a high, frosted window. I banged my fists against the wooden door. "Let us out!" I screamed.

"Monty," Nan said in a hushed voice. "Over here. Quick!"

I turned round. Nan was crouching by something in the corner. In the dim light it resembled a pile of old rags.

Then it moved. Groaned. Sat up.

Light fell on a pale face.

I cried out in shock.

"Uncle Leo!"

21

"Dad!" Nan cried. She reached out a hand to Uncle Leo.

Then she yanked it back.

"Dad—is it really you?" she whispered fearfully.

"It's really me. I promise," Uncle Leo replied weakly. He gazed from Nan to me. "So they got you too. I was afraid of this. I'm so sorry, kids."

Nan eyed him suspiciously. "If you're you— who's that man out there?"

Uncle Leo rubbed a hand wearily over his face. "He's a clone. They all are," he explained. "Human clones, grown in my lab."

I shivered. Even though I had guessed the truth, hearing it from Uncle Leo made it worse somehow.

"Why?" I cried. "Why did you clone me?"

Uncle Leo shook his head. "I didn't," he declared. "I would never clone another human being! Please believe me, Montgomery."

84

"Then how . . . ?" Nan stared at Uncle Leo. "I don't get it, Dad."

"I would never experiment on *another* human being. But I did experiment on myself," Uncle Leo explained. "Several months ago, I succeeded in cloning myself. It was an incredible breakthrough."

"Several months ago?" Nan gasped. "You mean there have been two of you running around for the last few months?"

"Not running around," Uncle Leo corrected. "I explained to my clone the importance of staying hidden in my lab—until we were ready to show him to the world. I thought he understood and agreed."

He heaved a deep sigh. "But what I didn't realize was that my clone is insane—insane and evil."

"Evil?" I echoed. I felt a cold knot in my stomach.

"I don't know what other word to use," Uncle Leo continued. *"He's* the one who cloned you, Montgomery. I think he took DNA samples from you last summer, when you and your mother came to visit. He sneaked out of the lab and into your bedroom in the middle of the night. I caught him in the hall, but he claimed he was simply taking a walk because he couldn't sleep."

I gasped. I had a sudden memory of the horrible nightmare from that night. The one where the man was scraping at my skin with a scalpel.

But it wasn't a nightmare at all. If Uncle Leo was right, it had really happened!

"So when you pricked Monty with that pin, you weren't taking DNA samples, were you, Dad?" Nan asked.

"Of course not!" Uncle Leo sounded shocked. "My goodness, that was just an accident. I certainly didn't mean to do it."

"I told you," Nan declared.

"Yeah, well . . ." I muttered. You couldn't blame me for being suspicious.

After all, I wasn't that far from the truth!

Uncle Leo put a hand on my shoulder. "I'm sorry. I would have stopped my clone—if only I had known. But it never crossed my mind that he might be lying to me. Why should he? It would be like me lying to myself." He sighed again. "Or that's what I thought in the beginning.

"Anyway," he continued, "as I continued running tests on my clone, I grew more and more worried. I began to suspect that there was something wrong with his mind. Something twisted."

I jumped up impatiently and began to pace back and forth. I wanted to get to the important part.

"But what about the clones of me?" I demanded.

"Leo Two was making them all along, in

secret," Uncle Leo told me. "He worked at night, while I slept. And he hid the Montgomery clones in the spare bedrooms so I wouldn't find them."

"No way!" Nan cried. "You mean I was sleeping next door to clones of Monty all this time?"

I shuddered. It was a horrible picture. While Nan and Uncle Leo and I went about our lives, these copies of me watched us . . . spied on us . . .

"I didn't find out about the Montgomery clones until two days ago," Uncle Leo told us. He turned to me. "When you described a boy who looked exactly like you, I began to wonder. Could Leo Two have been continuing my work behind my back?

"I went into the lab that night to confront him. To my horror, I found several Montgomery clones in there with him. When I threatened to stop them, they overpowered me. They locked me up in here."

He shook his head. "The only reason I'm still alive is because they think they need me. My scientific knowledge."

He fell silent. We all sat there for a moment in the dark closet. I didn't know what to say.

"Dad, isn't there any way to tell these clones apart from real people?" Nan demanded at last. "I mean, how do I know you're not really just another clone? Or Monty?"

"Hey!" I protested. "I'm no clone. I'm me!"

"How do I know that?" Nan challenged.

Uncle Leo leant his head back against the wall. "It's a good question," he sighed. "Of course, I needed a way to tell a clone from its original. So I made sure each clone had a tiny flaw."

He held up his right hand. "Each of the clones has a small blue dot here on the tip of his right thumb," he explained. "It looks like a tattoo, but it's not. It's more like a birthmark. It can't be removed."

Uncle Leo shook his head. "There is another difference between the clones and their originals," he added. "I don't know why, or how, but all of the clones are evil. They take pleasure in doing harm to other people."

"But what do they want? Why did Leo Two make so many clones of me?" I asked. "What are they planning to do?"

"Leo Two uses those clones of you as his personal slaves," Uncle Leo said. "The more, the better. He could never have overpowered me without them.

"But I don't know what they're planning," he admitted. "Whatever they're up to, it's bad."

He climbed stiffly to his feet. "Kids, we have to find some way to get out of here. We have to stop them somehow!"

CLICK! I heard a key turn in the lock behind me.

Heart pounding, I whirled round. The door

swung open. I squinted in the bright light.

Two clones of me stood in the doorway.

"Come here, Monty. We need you," one of them commanded. He grabbed my arm.

"No!" I yelled. I twisted my arm, trying to pull free. But I couldn't shake off his grip. And the clone didn't even seem to be straining.

He might look like me, but he was a whole lot stronger!

He dragged me out of the closet. I struggled wildly, but it was no use.

"What do you want?" I cried. My voice shook. "What are you going to do to me?"

"Let me go!" I screamed. "What are you doing?"

The clone gripped me tighter. "You'll find out," he promised.

"Nooooo!" I threw myself backwards, thrashing as hard as I could. I kicked the clone in the shins. I twisted my head, trying to bite his hand.

"Nice try," he growled. "Monty, help me hold him."

The other three clones immediately stepped forward.

Oh, no! They *all* answered to my name!

The four of them dragged me to a stainless-steel lab table. It was covered with white paper—the kind doctors use to protect their examining tables. Leather straps hung from the four corners.

They're going to strap me down, I realized. Strap me down so I can't struggle—while they do something horrible to me!

90

"Stop! Please!" I begged. But they hoisted me on to the table.

The Uncle Leo clone stepped forward and peered down at me as I lay there, helpless. He held up something that looked like a ballpoint pen. But at the tip I saw a long, shining needle.

Three of the Monty clones stepped back. The remaining one grabbed my right hand and spread it out.

The Uncle Leo clone flipped a tiny switch on the side of the pen. It began to buzz. The silver needle vibrated.

He lowered it to my right hand.

"No!" I shrieked. "Noooooo!"

I watched in horror as the needle touched the tip of my thumb.

Burning pain shot through my hand.

The Uncle Leo clone lifted the buzzing needle away.

I raised my head and stared down at my hand.

Stared down at a small blue dot tattooed on my right thumb.

My head fell back against the table. And my eyes met those of the Monty clone who held me down.

"There," he said softly. "Now you're just like us, Monty."

I closed my eyes, shuddering.

With the blue dot on my thumb, there was no way to prove that I wasn't a clone.

How am I going to get out of this? I wondered desperately.

"Unstrap him," the Uncle Leo clone commanded. "Let him sit up. He won't struggle any more."

The Monty clones began to unbuckle the leather straps that held my arms and legs.

Out of the corner of my eye I saw the door to the supply closet slowly inch open. The clones must have forgotten to lock it.

Nan peeked round the edge of the door. She met my gaze.

And I knew what I had to do. I had to keep their attention away from Nan.

As soon as my legs were free, I kicked out at two of the clones. I yelled and screamed like a maniac. I thrashed around on the table.

"Hold him down!" the Leo clone commanded sharply.

"I thought you said he wouldn't struggle any more!" one of the Monty clones yelled.

He tried to grab my shoulders. I snapped my teeth at his hand.

On the other side of the room, I caught a glimpse of Nan. She was creeping towards the lab door. She was almost there!

I struggled harder. "Let go of me!"

"He's too stupid to realize he can't escape. These originals are all so stupid," the Leo clone snapped.

"I'm not stupid!" I shouted. "You're the one who's stupid. You're just a dumb clone!"

"Watch your mouth, Monty," one of the Monty clones warned. "You don't know what you're talking about."

I didn't reply. I turned to the lab door. Nan had opened it. She was sneaking out.

One of the Monty clones spun to the door.

Too late! He was just in time to see Nan's red braid vanish as she hurried out.

"The girl!" the clone shouted furiously. "She got out!"

"Run, Nan!" I screamed at the top of my lungs. "Run!"

Three of the clones raced after Nan.

The other one stared down at me. "That was stupid, Monty," he told me. "She won't get away.

We'll catch her. You two don't want to make Uncle Leo angry. Uncle Leo can be *mean* when he's angry."

My skin prickled. But I tried to look as if I wasn't scared.

"She *will* get away," I declared. "You clones are history."

"Us?" My clone laughed. "What about you? Don't forget, you're one of us now. *Monty*."

"No!" I shouted. "No way!"

I sat there, feeling helpless.

How was I going to get out of this?

The minutes ticked by. The clones didn't return with Nan. My hopes began to rise.

Did she escape? Was she bringing help?

All I could do was wait.

After about half an hour, I heard a knock on the lab door.

"Who's there?" the Leo clone barked.

"It's Monty," a voice called through the door.

I shuddered. I would never get used to that!

A clone hurried over and unlocked the door. The other three clones stepped inside.

Without Nan.

"Where's the girl?" the Leo clone demanded.

"She got away," one of my clones admitted.

"We couldn't find her anywhere," another one said. "She's gone."

"Yes!" I cheered.

The Leo clone scowled. "That's bad," he muttered. He gnawed on his thumb. "Bad."

"Don't worry about it," one of my clones scoffed. "What can she do to us? She's just a dumb original."

"Who would believe her story anyway?" another clone added.

I felt cold. The clones were right. How could Nan ever convince a grown-up that she was telling the truth?

The Leo clone stretched and yawned. "I was up all night working—and all day looking after you brats. I'm going to take a nap."

He headed for a narrow bed in a corner of the lab. He lay down and closed his eyes. In seconds, he was snoring softly.

I sneezed.

As if they were one person, all of my clones turned to stare at me.

Then they began to move slowly towards me.

My breath caught in my throat.

What were they thinking? What did they want?

I jumped up from the lab table. I backed away from the clones until I was pressed against the wall.

The clones moved closer.

"What's the matter?" one of them asked. "You aren't shy, are you, Monty?"

"Yeah. Are you, Monty?" another one jeered.

I hated the way they kept repeating my name. There was something so creepy about it!

"Leave me alone!" I cried shrilly. "Just leave me alone!"

They laughed. *My* laugh.

"After a while you'll get used to being part of a group," another of the clones said.

"But I'm *not!*" I declared. My heart thumped. "I'm me!"

"No, *I'm* you," one of them corrected me.

"No, *I'm* you," another one insisted.

"No, *I'm* you!"

"*I'm* you!"

I stared from one identical face to the other. I felt a buzzing in my ears. This is insane, I thought. Insane!

Then one of the clones held up his hand.

"Initiation time," he announced.

24

"Initiation?" I cried weakly.

"It's just a little test," a clone told me.

Two of them grabbed me. They dragged me to the worktop piled high with Uncle Leo's electrical equipment.

"No!" I cried. "Stop! Leave me alone!"

One of them pulled a box of wooden matches out of a drawer. He struck a match, then lit a Bunsen burner. A blue flame rose up in front of me.

"Ready, Monty?" he asked.

"Ready, Monty?" the other three clones chorused.

"No!" I yelled. "Please!"

Two of them held me so I couldn't struggle.

A third grabbed my hand—and forced it into the blue flame!

"Yaaaiii!" I screamed.

The fire seared my palm.

I snatched my hand away. And stared down at it.

The skin on my palm was burned red.

"What are you trying to do—kill me?" I cried. "What do you want?"

"Watch," one of the clones said.

He held his hand up in front of my face. Then, smiling, he stuck it into the flame.

And held it there.

"What are you doing?" I gasped. "Are you *crazy*?"

The clone pulled his hand back. "See?" he said. "It doesn't hurt me."

"Or me," one of the other clones chimed in. He stuck *his* hand into the flame.

"Or me," the third one called.

"Or me," the fourth one added.

"Don't you get it? We don't feel pain. We're *better* than you, Monty," the first clone said. "Smarter. Stronger. We're an improvement!"

I cried out in horror.

I had to get away from these frightening clones!

I yanked my arms free and dived for the lab door. I threw myself at it, wrestling with the bolt.

The clones grabbed me and pulled me back. "No way," one of them scolded. "You're staying with us!"

"Then lock me up!" I demanded. "Lock me up with Uncle Leo if I'm your prisoner!"

"You don't get it, do you?" The clone folded his arms. "You're in the group now, Monty. In fact, call *me* Monty. Because I'm you. I'm taking your life. And do you know what I'm going to call *you*?"

I couldn't speak. I simply shook my head.

The clone leant close. "Nothing," he whispered. "You're just a clone."

Just a clone. The words echoed in my head. *Just a clone.*

"Are you asleep yet, Monty?" one of the clones whispered in the darkness.

I was awake. But I lay quiet and didn't answer.

First of all, he probably wasn't talking to me.

Second, I wanted them all to think I was sleeping. Then maybe *they'd* fall asleep—and I could escape.

There were no windows in the lab. But I was pretty sure it was dark outside. Nan had been gone for hours already.

Where is she? I wondered. She probably can't get anyone to help her. Or believe her.

I knew she was still trying. But what if she failed?

It's up to me to get out of here, I realized. To help Nan. To rescue Uncle Leo.

I strained my ears in the darkness. Were they awake?

All I could hear was steady breathing.

They're sleeping, I decided. They must be!

Now or never, Monty!

As silently as I could, I sat up. I swung my legs over the edge of the bed. Then I used my hands to push myself up.

Yow! I bit my lip to keep from crying in pain. My burned palm throbbed.

I stood there for a second, catching my breath, waiting for the pain to fade.

No time to waste. I tiptoed to the lab door. I grasped the bolt and began to work it gently back and forth.

My heart pounded. Would they wake up?

The bolt wiggled under my hand.

Yes! I wanted to cheer.

I was almost out!

Almost free!

One more second. One more second and I'm out!

The lights flickered on.

I froze in terror.

Slowly, I turned round.

The four clones stood in a ring around me. The Leo clone rose up behind them, glaring at me.

"Going somewhere?" he demanded.

"I—I—" I sputtered.

"We're very light sleepers," one of the clones said. "I told you before, Monty, we're *better* than you. Don't think you can—"

BAM! BAM! BAM!

Loud blows rang out. The lab door! I jumped away.

The door flew open. Nan burst in—followed by three men.

They all appeared to be about Uncle Leo's age. They wore rumpled suits. Two were plump and balding. The third was tall and broad-shouldered—but his glasses were even thicker than Uncle Leo's.

"*This* is the help you brought?" I choked out.

But no one paid any attention to me. The

101

men's eyes were practically popping out as they stared at the clones.

The tall man turned to the Leo clone.

"Leo!" he cried. "What's going on?"

"Who are you?" the Leo clone demanded angrily. "What right do you have to burst into my lab like this?"

"That's not my dad!" Nan cried. "He didn't even recognize his old college room-mates. He's the clone! Grab him!"

The three men exchanged glances.

Then the two plump ones stepped forward and seized the Leo clone by the arms!

"All right!" I cheered.

"Let's get him out to the truck," the tall man said. They began to haul the Leo clone out of the room.

The Leo clone's face was beet-red. "This is outrageous!" he cried. "Outrageous!"

I glanced at my clones. I waited for them to help the Leo clone.

But they did nothing. They just stood there, watching in silence.

Why? I wondered uneasily.

What are they planning?

Nan ran across the room. She turned the key in the lock of the supply closet. "Dad!" she called.

Uncle Leo stumbled out, blinking in the light.

"Nan!" he exclaimed, embracing her. "Are you all right?"

"I'm fine," Nan declared. "I brought your college room-mates, Dad."

"I'm so glad you lot are here!" Uncle Leo cried. "I wrote to you last week because I was afraid my experiments were spinning out of control!"

"I tried to find help, but no one would believe me," Nan explained. "Not even the police! So I hid in the garage and waited for your friends to come."

"But what are they going to do?" I asked.

"They're going to deal with the clones," Nan replied. "They're setting up a special lab in South America. Soon the clones will be far away."

"I can't wait," I said. "Nan, I'm so glad you're back. I was beginning to think something had happened to you!"

I was so relieved that I reached out to hug her.

She jerked away. "Don't touch me!"

I stared at her in shock. "But—"

"I don't know who you are!" Nan said sharply. "You could be one of *them*."

"Nan!" I couldn't believe it. "Don't you recognize me? Can't you tell the difference?"

"Don't listen to him!" one of my clones cried. "He's trying to trick you. *I'm* the real Monty!"

"They're both lying!" another one declared. "It's me!"

Nan's eyes narrowed. "Let me see your right

thumbs." The tattoo! She would see the tattoo!

Fear gripped me. I slowly held out my right hand.

So did my clones.

"You don't understand," I said miserably. "They tattooed me. We're all the same now."

Nan's eyes widened as she stared at all our thumbs.

Uncle Leo frowned. "That *is* a problem."

The men came back into the room. "Leo!" the tall one exclaimed. "Is that really you?"

"Fred!" Uncle Leo grabbed the man's hand and shook it. "Thank goodness you three got here in time!"

"Barely," one of the short, bald men pointed out. He waved a hand around at me and all the clones. "Which one is your nephew?"

"That's the trouble," Uncle Leo murmured. "We aren't sure."

"It's no problem at all," one of my clones announced.

I stared at him. "What do you mean? It's a big problem!"

"No, it isn't," the clone declared. "I can prove I'm the real Monty!"

"How?" one of Uncle Leo's room-mates asked.

"I know things no copy could possibly know," the clone announced.

He turned to Nan. "Remember what I told you the other night? About what happened when we were seven? How we both stole parts of Evan Seymour's train set? I got the engine, and you got the caboose?"

"And we never told anyone else," Nan said slowly.

I gasped. That night when Nan and I were talking—the clone must have been listening to us the whole time!

"Hey!" I yelled. "That's *my* story! I'm the one who told you that story, Nan! Not him! Don't believe him!"

"No! I am!" one of the other clones shouted.

"Liar! I am!"

"No! I am!"

I clapped my hands over my ears to shut out the noise. "It was me!" I shouted. "I told you that story. Me! *I'm* Monty!"

Nan stepped forward.

"I believe you," she said softly. "You're really Monty."

And she held out her hand—to the clone.

"Noooo!" I howled. "No! Nan! You can't do this!"

"Nan!" the other three clones shrieked. "Don't you know me?"

Nan shook her head. "Let's go," she begged Uncle Leo.

He nodded. "You and Montgomery go on. We'll bring the clones out to the truck. The sooner we get them out of the house, the better."

Nan and the clone hurried out of the lab. Then the four men each grabbed hold of one of us. They hustled us through the house. Out to a white removal van that stood in the driveway.

They opened the rear doors and shoved us in. The clones struggled and yelled—but I couldn't. I was in a daze of horror.

My own twin sister couldn't recognize me! She thought I was a clone!

What was I going to do now?

How was I going to get out of this?

The inside of the truck was fitted with two rows of plastic seats, bolted to the floor.

The Leo clone huddled in one of the corner seats, muttering to himself.

I heard the murmur of voices outside as Uncle Leo and his friends discussed what to do next. I caught little snatches of sentences—"ship leaves tomorrow morning" and "warehouse by the river".

Fred, the tall man, stuck his head in. "Buckle up," he advised us. "We're about to get moving."

Then he slammed the rear doors. We were locked in.

I chose a seat and strapped on my seat-belt. The clones did the same.

The truck started up. We rode in silence.

Think. Think. Think! I ordered myself. I had to find a way out of this—before I ended up in a lab in South America!

About fifteen minutes later, the truck stopped. Outside, I heard the whine of big machines and the beep of trucks as they backed up. Where were we? I wondered.

"Sounds like a loading dock," one of my clones remarked.

"We're at the river," another one added.

"They'll load us on the ship to South America in the morning," a third one said.

The little window between the back of the

truck and the cab slid open. Fred peered out at us.

"We'll be here a while," he told us. "Might as well make yourselves comfortable. And in case you have any ideas about trying to escape— we're posting a guard outside the truck."

A guard! I slumped down in my seat in despair.

I knew this was my last chance to escape. Once they put me on that ship to South America, I was history. There was no way I could get back.

I would spend the rest of my life as a lab experiment!

But how could I escape?

I gazed round the inside of the truck. The window into the cab was too small to wriggle through. And the doors looked far too solid to break down. Besides, a guard stood outside.

I glanced up.

And saw it. A hatch in the ceiling.

A sliding hatch, open a crack.

Could I escape through the top of the truck?

The ceiling of the truck was far over my head. How could I reach the hatch?

Could I stack up some of the plastic seats and climb up on them?

No. They were bolted to the floor.

I swallowed hard. There was only one thing to do.

I had to ask my clones for help.

"Hey," I began. My voice squeaked.

I cleared my throat and tried again. "Hey. We can get out if we work together. How about it—uh, Monty? Will you help me?"

My clones all stared at me.

"Why should I help you?" one of them demanded. "*I'm* Monty. You're the one that should be helping *me*."

"No, *I'm* Monty," the second one objected.

"No, *I* am!" the third one cried. "You should all help me!"

The Leo clone glared at us from his corner. "Pipe down," he snapped. "I'm sick of all this arguing. You're *all* Monty."

That was when I got an idea. A really smart idea.

"Listen to me!" I called over the noise. "Uncle Leo is right. We *are* all the same!"

The clones stopped yelling and stared at me again.

"Let's face it—we're all clones and we know it," I went on. "Why are we trying to fool each other? That dumb original is back there, living *our* life, while we get shipped off to some lab. Is that right? Is that fair?"

"No!" the clones shouted.

"He's just an original!" one of them added. "We're better than him!"

"Right!" I yelled. "So I say let's work together.

Let's all get out of this truck—and then go back to the house and get rid of him. This is all his fault anyway."

"Yeah!"

"Let's go!"

Yes! I had to struggle to keep a smile from spreading over my face. I suppose we originals aren't so dumb after all! I thought.

"Okay, here's how we're going to do it," I began. I grabbed one of the clones and pulled him to the middle of the truck, underneath the hatch. "Stand here, Monty."

Next I pointed at a second clone. "You—climb on Monty's shoulders. Then the other Monty here will help me get on *your* shoulders. I'll climb out the hatch up there and find some rope to lower down to you lot. Got it?"

"Got it, Monty," the clones replied.

Of course, there was no way I'd lower any rope down to them. Once I was out, it would be "So long, suckers!" In fact, I planned to bolt the hatch from the outside as soon as I was through. Just to make sure they couldn't escape.

Two of the clones made a kind of human ladder for me. The third one boosted me up on to the second one's shoulders. The Leo clone sat in the corner, watching.

Cautiously, I reached for the edge of the hatch.

"Go on, Monty!" one of the clones cheered. "You can do it!"

"Got it!" I grunted. I slid the hatch open. Then I felt around the edges of the hatch for a handhold.

I felt a sudden sharp pain in my index finger. "Ow!" I yelped, jerking my hand back. I must have jabbed it on a nail or something.

Below me, there was sudden silence.

Then the Leo clone yelled, "He's the original! Get him!"

Oh, no!

The clones don't feel pain! I remembered. I gave myself away!

Before I could move, hands seized my ankles.

They grabbed me—and pulled me down on to the floor of the truck.

"Nooo!" I hit the metal floor feet first and rolled. *WHAM!* My head slammed into the corner of one of the plastic seats.

"Ohhh," I moaned. I huddled on the floor, clutching my head. I closed my eyes in pain.

When I opened them again, three identical faces were glaring into mine. The Leo clone towered over them.

"You lied to us, Monty," one of my clones said softly. "We don't like that."

"We don't like *you*, Monty," another one added. "We don't like anything about you."

111

My throat closed up with fear.

"Wh-wh-what are you going to do to me?" I stammered.

"What you said we should do," he told me. "We're going to get rid of you, Monty."

Three pairs of hands reached out for me.

27

"Wait!" I pleaded. "Can't we talk about this?"

"What is there to talk about, Monty?" one of the clones demanded.

"Yeah, Monty. What could you possibly have to say to us?" another asked.

"You're a loser, Monty," the third one sneered.

Why do they keep repeating my name? I wondered desperately.

And then I got my second idea.

It was a long shot. But at least it might distract them while I thought of a better plan.

"You hate the name Monty, don't you?" I asked.

The clones paused.

"Well, I mean, who wouldn't?" I continued. "It's a terrible name. That's what you hate about me the most."

"So?" one of them demanded.

"At least let me pick another name before I

die," I urged. "Like Pete, maybe. I always wanted to be called Pete."

"Pete?" the first clone repeated.

"Yeah. Pete Adams. Sounds good, don't you think?" I forced a smile.

The second clone sat back on his heels. "Yeah. Pete," he declared. "It has a ring to it. I like it!"

"No way!" another clone protested. "Pete is boring. What about Ferris?"

Ferris! I tried not to make a face. "Yeah, that's good too," I said.

"Ferris! That's even worse than Monty!" the first clone jeered. "What are you—a total geek?"

The third clone scrambled to his feet. "Who are you calling a geek, Monty?"

"Don't call me Monty!" the first clone yelled. "I hate that name! I'm Pete!"

"No, *I'm* Pete!" the second clone cried.

"No, I am!" the first one insisted.

"Let's get on with this," the Leo clone snapped. "Forget this silly name business."

"Don't call me Monty!" a third clone shouted. "I'm Ferris!"

"You're a bonehead!" another clone exclaimed nastily.

"Aaargh!" another clone screeched—and dived angrily at the other two.

In a moment the three of them were rolling on the floor. Kicking. Punching. Yelling.

"Oh, wonderful," the Leo clone grumbled. He retreated to a corner seat and stared unhappily at the floor.

Now was my chance.

"Help!" I screamed. "Help!"

"Hey!" a voice called from outside the truck. "What's going on in there?"

The guard! He heard me!

"Help me—please!" I cried.

The clones paid no attention. They were too busy fighting one another.

The rear doors of the truck flew open. A tall, powerful-looking man with curly black hair stood in the opening. "What's all the noise?" he demanded.

His eyes widened as he took in the three clones. Then his gaze shifted to me.

"What is this?" he gasped. "Quadruplets? A circus act?"

I've never thought faster in my life.

"You have to stop them!" I yelled. "My brothers—they're killing each other!"

"Okay, kids. Break it up. Break it up!" the guard bellowed.

Now was my chance.

Heart pounding, I pushed past the guard—and leapt out of the back of the truck.

I gazed round. We were at some kind of loading dock on the river. It was late at night, but giant floodlights made the place as bright as day. Huge cranes whined around me, hoisting metal containers in and out of ships.

"Hey!" I heard the guard cry. "Come back here! Hey—somebody stop that kid!"

I ran as fast as I could. I never glanced back.

I didn't know where I was going. I just knew I had to get away.

Heavy feet pounded after me. I dodged behind a stack of huge metal containers.

"Where did he go?" someone yelled.

As quietly as I could, I doubled back the other way.

I worked my way away from the river's edge. Keeping to the shadows. Freezing every time I heard a voice or a footstep. Running across the open spaces as fast as I could.

I found myself at the entrance to the docks. A tall chain-link fence towered above me. Big trucks rumbled past.

A green highway sign read PHILADELPHIA 28. MORTONVILLE 8. The arrow for Mortonville pointed to the left.

I was eight miles from Uncle Leo's house.

I glanced back. No one seemed to be following me.

Still sticking to the shadows, I stepped out on to the road and began to walk. Eight miles. With luck, I would be home in time for breakfast . . .

I walked all night. A red sun was just peeking

116

over the roofs of the houses as I made my way up to Uncle Leo's house.

My shirt was rumpled and drenched in sweat. My khakis were stained with mud.

Trembling all over, I sneaked a peek into the kitchen window. I could see Nan, Uncle Leo and my clone. My clone, sitting at the breakfast table as if he belonged there!

I ducked away. And made my way to the front porch.

In a few seconds, I'd be facing him, facing the boy Nan mistook for me. The boy who stole my life.

I had to take my life back. I had to prove to Nan and Uncle Leo that I am the real Monty.

But how?

How?

Swallowing hard, my heart thumping in my chest, I rang the doorbell.

28

"Was that the doorbell?" I asked.

"I didn't hear anything, Nan," Monty replied. He tapped a spoon against his empty cereal bowl. "Pass the Frosted Flakes."

I stared out of the kitchen window. Morning sunlight streamed into the room.

I hadn't slept much all night. I couldn't stop thinking about the horrors of yesterday. Those evil clones.

Thank goodness it's over, I thought with a sigh. I hope those clones are on their way to South America. Dad, Monty and I won't feel safe until they are far away.

"Nan—the cereal please," Monty repeated.

"Oh. Sorry," I murmured. "I was think-ing . . ."

"Don't think about it any more, Nan," Dad said. "It was a frightening thing. Now we have to go on with our lives."

I passed the cereal to Monty and then pulled

a sugar doughnut from the bag on the table. "Mmmm." Soft and fresh.

The doorbell rang.

"I *did* hear the doorbell!" I exclaimed.

"I'll get it." Monty jumped up and hurried out of the kitchen.

I heard him open the front door. And then I heard shouting.

"What are you doing here?" Monty cried. "Get away from here!"

"What in the world?" Dad rose from his chair.

Loud, hurried footsteps. Then Monty burst breathlessly back into the kitchen.

Followed by—Monty!

I jumped up. My heart skipped a beat. I stared from one to the other.

The first Monty wore a blue-and-white-striped soccer jersey and faded jeans. The second Monty wore a mud-stained pair of khakis and a torn, rumpled, sweaty blue shirt.

"He escaped from the truck!" the first Monty cried. "He's a clone!"

"Listen to me," the second one gasped. *"He's* the clone! I'm Monty! You were wrong yesterday, Nan. You have to believe me!"

Oh wow, I thought. My head started to spin. I dropped back into my chair.

The nightmare—it's starting again . . .

"I won't let you do this!" the first Monty cried.

"You have to go to South America with the others. You can't steal my life!"

"*Your* life!" the second one choked out. "It's mine!"

With a desperate cry, he threw himself on the first Monty. The two boys wrestled on the kitchen floor, punching each other, rolling over and over.

I pressed my hands to my face and watched them fight. "Dad—what are we going to do?" I cried.

"I don't know how to solve this," he sighed. "I don't know how to tell them apart!"

I snapped my fingers.

"I do," I said. "I have an idea."

I picked up the doughnut bag from the breakfast table. I pulled out two doughnuts. "Stop fighting!" I screamed. "Stop it right now. I know how to solve this."

To my surprise, they stopped wrestling. They pulled apart, breathing hard.

My heart was pounding. I hope this works! I thought.

I handed them each a doughnut. "Go ahead. Eat it," I instructed them. "Remember what happened last time? In a few seconds we'll know which one is really Monty."

Both Montys hesitated.

"Go on. Do it," I insisted.

One Monty shrugged. Then he bit into the doughnut.

The second Monty hesitated a moment longer. "I wish there was another way," he muttered.

Then he bit into his doughnut too.

I waited with my arms crossed. Dad stared at them over the top of his glasses.

I glanced at the kitchen clock. It seemed as if each second took an hour.

And then—"*Brrraaaagh!*"

The first Monty pitched forward. And vomited all over the kitchen floor.

"Monty!" I shrieked. I threw my arms around him. I didn't even care that he was still puking. "I knew it was you!" I cried.

"Very clever, Nan!" Dad said, smiling. "But you took a chance. No one is sure exactly how allergies work. The clone might have been allergic to peanut oil too."

I chuckled, still hugging my brother. "Good thing I don't know anything about allergies!"

The Monty clone snarled with rage. "It's a trick!" he fumed.

"That's enough out of you," Dad growled. He seized the clone by his shirt collar. "You're going back to the truck! You can wait in my lab until Fred and the others come for you."

"You're wrong!" the clone howled. "He's the clone. I'm telling you, *he's the clone!*"

"You just won't give up—will you!" I declared.

Dad dragged the clone away. Monty and I hurried to get paper towels to clean up the mess.

That evening, Monty and I were sprawled on the rug in front of the television. We were sharing a big bowl of popcorn, watching a stupid *Police Academy* movie.

"The ship with the clones must be on its way to South America by now," Monty said.

I shivered. "I'm so glad they're out of our lives! Wasn't it smart of me to think of that doughnut test?"

Monty rolled over on to his side. "I was even smarter," he said softly.

"Huh?" I stared at him.

"I switched the doughnuts before you woke up," he said. "I bought baked doughnuts instead of fried. So there was no peanut oil in them."

"But—but I don't understand!" I stammered. "You got sick, Monty! You threw up!"

He shrugged. "I faked it. I've been practising for weeks."

My heart skipped a beat. I pulled myself up to my knees. "You mean *you're* the clone?" My whole body was trembling. "And we sent the real Monty to South America?"

"You're slow," he sneered. "But you've got it now."

"But how?" I gasped. "How did you do it? How did you know about the doughnuts—and everything else?"

"I overheard a lot of stuff," he replied. "Like that stupid story about how you two stole birthday presents. And I was hiding outside the kitchen window when he ate that doughnut and puked all over the place."

I felt cold all over. "How could you?" I moaned. "How could you do that to poor Monty?"

The clone grinned at me. A wide, cruel grin.

"Nan," he whispered in my ear. "I'm your evil twin!"